D0537609

# Stinky Finger's
## Deadly Doll
### of Death

Also by Jon Blake,
published by Hodder Children's Books:

*The Deadly Secret of Dorothy W.*
*The Mad Mission of Jasmin J.*

And more adventures
with Stinky and friends:

*Stinky Finger's House of Fun*
*Stinky Finger's Crazy Party*
*Stinky Finger's Mystery Guest*
*Stinky Finger's Holiday Mania*
*Stinky Finger's Peace and Love Thing*

Visit Jon Blake's website at:
www.jonblake.co.uk

# Stinky Finger's

## Deadly Doll
## of Death

# Jon Blake

illustrated by
**David Roberts**

*Hodder
Children's
Books*

A division of Hachette Children's Books

Hodder Children's Books
A division of Hachette Children's Books
338 Euston Road, London NW1 3BH
An Hachette Livre UK company

# Before We Begin

Greetings. I am Blue Soup, your storyteller. Reports that I no longer exist are totally untrue. They were spread by an intergalactic anorak called Dave who posed as my replacement, Blue Soup 2.0. I must warn anyone who has been in contact with this supposed narrator that he carries a parasite called the !"£$%^^&* Worm, which burrows beneath your fingernails and causes you to send out random embarrassing emails to friends and family, even if you haven't got a computer and don't know how to use one.

I don't just tell stories. I make everything work on Earth, though quite why, or how, you will never know. As you may have heard, I come from Outer Space. Beyond the very last star, in fact.

I was brought here by the Spoonheads. The Spoonheads are what you call aliens, except to them, you are aliens, and pretty weird ones at that.

Anyway, on to our story. This is the sixth story of Stinky Finger, who was first described in Stinky Finger's House of Fun. There are no grown-ups in Stinky's world. They've all been sucked up into the Space Zoo by the Spoonheads. That's why Stinky and his friends are in charge of the House of Fun, where wild adventures are around every corner … as you will soon discover.

# Chapter One

Never had the House of Fun known such a storm. The wind tore at the slates, rain lashed at the windows, hailstones hammered at the doors, and sleet judo-chopped the chimneys. Icky and Stinky sat at the kitchen table playing battleships, while Bryan sat under it, repeating "We're all going to die," non-stop, for seven hours.

"Three hundred and twenty-nine X," said Stinky.

"Miss," replied Icky.

Stinky frowned. "Do we have to have so many squares?" he groaned.

"Got anything better to do?" asked Icky.

Stinky shook his head.

"Two hundred and fifty-three P," said Icky.

"Hit," said Stinky.

"Hit?" said Icky. "Frabjous! You mean I've actually found your battleship?"

"Yes, well done," said Stinky. "Er ... did you say B, or P?"

"P," replied Icky.

"Oh," said Stinky. "In that case it's a miss."

Icky sighed. "I think you've ruined the game, Stinky," he said.

"Have I?" asked Stinky. "Why's that?"

"Never mind," said Icky.

"We're all going to die," mumbled Bryan.

"For Pete's sake, Bryan!" cried Icky. "Stop—"

The rest of Icky's words were drowned out by a giant crack of thunder and a flash of lightning which lit the kitchen like a firework. There was an almighty crash somewhere above them, followed soon after by another great thud outside the front door.

"See!?" cried Bryan. "The house is collapsing!"

"It did sound like a chimney," agreed Stinky.

"Let's go and find out," replied Icky, leaping to his feet.

There was an even louder crack of thunder, and Icky sat down again. "Maybe wait a while," he said.

"What shall we play now?" asked Stinky.

"How about General Knowledge?" suggested Icky.

"A capital idea!" cried Bryan, his beady eyes suddenly appearing from beneath the table. "We're still going to die though," he added quickly.

"What is a doxiepoo?" asked Icky.

Bryan's face fell. It was one of the three words he'd never heard of.

"Is it a poodle crossed with a sausage dog?" asked Stinky.

"Brilliant!" cried Icky. "How did you get that, Stinky?"

"You ask me it every day," replied Stinky.

Icky looked sheepish. "Do I?" he asked.

"Around breakfast-time usually," replied Stinky.

Icky looked even more sheepish. "I just like the word," he muttered.

"That question didn't count," snapped Bryan. "Ask another."

"Has it stopped raining?" asked Stinky.

This was an unexpected but well-chosen question, to which the answer, surprisingly, was "yes", although Bryan was unwilling to give it, as it possibly meant they weren't going to die after all. Icky didn't answer either, but only because he was half way to the front door.

As quickly as the storm had begun, so it had ended. The rain had stopped, the wind died down and the dark clouds lifted to reveal a full-fun sun. All the chimneys of the House of Fun were intact, and all that lay outside the front door was a toy pedal car which Stinky had unwisely left on the roof.

12

Stinky and Bryan joined Icky at the front door, and the three housemates breathed in the new-mown fresh-washing tasty-dirt smell you always get after rain. Life was good, even though, according to Bryan, it was still going to end soon.

Just then, who should come up the road but someone the housemates had never met before. He was a pale thin boy with a halo of pale red hair. Over one shoulder he carried a coil of wire and over the other a net.

"Hail fellow and well met," said Bryan, who had read Shakespeare and knew how to address strangers. "Pray, what is that you're carrying – is it a fishing net?"

The pale thin boy stopped, lowered his load and took a breath. "Not a fishing net," he replied. "A safety net."

The words "safety net" struck a dim memory in Stinky's mind. He'd heard of a safety match – maybe when you played in a safety match you scored into a safety net?

"Can we have it?" he asked.

"Get your own," replied the pale boy.

"Are there more?" asked Icky.

"There's tons of stuff," replied the boy. "High wires … clown costumes … jugglers' clubs … you name it."

"Where?" asked Icky, becoming ever-so-slightly excited.

"Dragon's Cove," replied the boy. "The *SS Entertainer*'s run aground."

"Gonk!" cried Icky. "A shipwreck!"

"You'd better be quick," replied the boy. "Half the town's there already." With that, he took up his load again and plodded off up the road.

"Wait!" cried Bryan. "Your name! You never told us your name!"

Without breaking step, the pale boy looked back over his shoulder. "Dandy Dinmont," he replied. "Mark it well."

Bryan made a mental note, but no one else need bother, as he isn't going to appear again in this story or any other.

"What are we waiting for?" asked Icky, and before anyone could reply, he was haring off down the road like a demented whippet.

# Chapter Two

Dragon's Cove had never seen anything like it. The *SS Entertainer* lay broken-backed on the rocks around the headland, and the beach was strewn with its cargo like a heavenly jumble sale. But for every crate, package or costume there was at least one boy or girl, and a steady trail of scavengers were leaving with booty. Some wore fantastic African masks, some carried boxes of firecrackers, and one group formed a wiggling Chinese dragon with a terrifying head.

The three housemates watched it all with frustrated eyes. They had all the dressing-up clothes they needed in the House of Fun, but the other tempting treats looked too good to miss.

"Maybe we could trade them something for that Chinese dragon," suggested Icky.

Stinky delved into his pocket and pulled out a hard grey-green object with strange irregular edges. "I've got this," he said.

Bryan took the object and examined it closely. "Is it moon rock?" he asked.

"No," replied Stinky. "Just my hanky."

Bryan shrieked and flung the horrible dried lump into the air. It dropped on the far side of some nearby rocks.

"My Aunt Hetty gave me that," said Stinky.

"We'll find it, Stinky," replied Icky.

The three housemates made their way over the rain-pocked sand and climbed on to the rocks. As they looked down on to a collection of pools, something caught Icky's eye. "Is that the corner of a box?" he said.

Sure enough, there was something wooden peeking out from behind a boulder. Forgetting Stinky's hanky entirely, they hurried to investigate. Wedged into a narrow crevice was a square crate, not much bigger than a person's head. With a few yanks it came free and sat before the housemates full of promise and mystery.

"Let's open it!" cried Icky, hands leaping for the catch which secured the lid.

"WAIT!" commanded Bryan.

"What for?" cried Icky.

"We have no idea what's inside that box," barked Bryan.

"That's why we want to open it!" replied Icky.

"It could be filled to the brim with tarantulas," declared Bryan.

"Don't be ridiculous," replied Icky.

Bryan stayed Icky's arm. His face was deadly serious. "This feeling I've been having," he pronounced. "It's very powerful."

"What feeling's that, Bryan?" asked Stinky.

"The feeling that one of us ... or all of us ... is going to die," replied Bryan.

"I thought that was because of the storm," said Icky.

"The storm was a red herring," replied Bryan.

Stinky watched Bryan's face for a considerable while, hoping to get some kind of clue as to Bryan's meaning. "No," he said, finally. "You've lost me there."

"I suggest we take the box home," replied Bryan, "dress ourselves in protective uniforms, and manipulate it with long-handled implements, having carried out a controlled explosion to open it."

"I suggest you're nuts," said Icky.

"OK," said Bryan. "We'll have a vote on it."

It was a surprise that Bryan said this. The housemates had had several hundred votes, and Bryan hadn't won one yet.

"OK," said Icky.

"Who doesn't want to die?" asked Bryan.

Bryan immediately raised his hand, followed quickly by Stinky.

"I win," declared Bryan. "Let's take the box home."

# Chapter Three

The preparations were all in place. The housemates hadn't been able to find any chemical warfare suits, so they'd put on deep sea diving gear instead. They didn't have any explosives either, so they'd rigged a bottle of Icky's home-made ginger beer to the crate. Something had gone wrong with Icky's ginger beer and it had started to ferment like real beer, so if you shook the bottles they exploded. According to Icky, however, this wasn't a mistake at all. They were bound to need to blow something up one day.

The housemates placed the crate at the front door, then retreated as far as possible down the hall. Bryan took hold of the long-handled multi-purpose lifting-and-shaking tool they had fashioned out of raspberry canes, litter-grabbers and long-nosed pliers.

"Everybody ready?" he asked, although it wasn't easy to hear him inside his deep-sea diving helmet.

Icky and Stinky prepared their catapults, primed to fire at tarantulas, black mambas, insane magicians' rabbits, or anything else that moved.

"Let's do it," said Bryan. With that, he lifted the ginger beer bottle with his lifting-and-shaking tool, and shook it.

Nothing happened.

"You haven't shaken it hard enough," said Icky.

"I've shaken it as hard as I can," replied Bryan.

"Go up to it and give it another shake with your hand," suggested Icky.

"Are you mad?" spluttered Bryan.

"You'll be safe," said Icky. "There's always a few seconds before it goes off."

"I really—" began Bryan.

# BLAMMMM!

It was carnage. The bottle was blown to smithereens, the lid of the crate was blasted clean off, and half the hallway was drenched in ginger beer.

"Gonk!" cried Icky.

"You … you would have killed me!" gasped Bryan.

"Like I said," replied Icky, "there's always a few seconds before it goes off."

Meanwhile, Stinky was quietly padding up the hall. He reached the open crate and took a peek inside.

*"Werrrrr!"* he cried, leaping back.

"What is it, Stinks?" yelled Icky.

"A face!" blurted Stinky. "A face looked up at me!"

"Is it human?" asked Icky, excitedly.

"I … I think so," stammered Stinky.

"Is it connected to a body?" asked Icky, even more excitedly.

"I … I don't know," burbled Stinky.

"Is it alive?" asked Bryan, fearfully.

"I … I'm not sure," stammered Stinky. "It does smell," he added, helpfully.

"What of?" asked Icky.

"Ginger beer," replied Stinky.

Icky could stand it no more. Heedless of any danger he galloped up the hallway and stared into the crate. His face immediately lit up with a shiny-eyed smile. "It's a doll!" he cried.

Stinky edged up behind him, followed closely by Bryan.

"That is no doll," pronounced Bryan. "That is a ventriloquist's dummy."

"How can you tell?" asked Icky.

"The mouth," replied Bryan. "It opens."

Icky lifted the doll-dummy out of the crate. It

had a shiny painted face and a permanent smiley mouth, which, just as Bryan had said, could open and close. The face sat on a pole which went down into a little body dressed in a dinner jacket and bow tie. At the back of the body was a convenient hole into which, as Icky soon discovered, an arm could be stuck.

"I think you're right, Bryan," said Icky. "It is a tiller-kiss dummy."

"What's a tiller-kiss dummy?" asked Stinky.

"*Ventriloquist's* dummy," corrected Bryan. "The dummy of a *ventriloquist*, a *ventriloquist* being a person who throws his or her voice. From the Latin *venter* and *loqui*, i.e. belly and speak."

"I hope I never meet one of those," said Stinky.

"Why do you say that?" asked Bryan.

"If that's his dummy," replied Stinky, "think how big his mouth is."

Icky thought about explaining, but was feeling slightly tired, so decided to demonstrate instead. Sitting the little man on his knee and pulling the cord that opened its mouth, Icky grit his teeth together, and in a strange high-pitched voice yelled "Gottle of geer!"

"I saw your lips move," said Bryan.

"What's 'gottle of geer'?" asked Stinky.

"I can't say Gee," replied Icky.

"You just said Gee," Stinky pointed out.

"Not *Gee*," replied Icky. "*Gee*. A, Gee, C!"

"I still saw your lips move," said Bryan.

"Let's see you do better," replied Icky.

"OK," said Bryan.

With a miffed frown, Icky handed the dummy to Bryan. But as Bryan lowered the dummy on to his lap, Icky's frown disappeared, to be replaced by huge gleeful smile. "It looks just like you!" he cried.

Bryan turned the dummy's face towards his own and pondered. "It is quite handsome I suppose," he replied.

"Put your spare glasses on it!" cried Icky.

Bryan actually had five pairs of spare glasses, one for every size print he might read, as he did read a lot. He selected one pair and fitted them on to the dummy. The effect was frabjous, gonk and ducks-deluxe all rolled into one.

"It's you!" cried Icky and Stinky, with one voice.

Bryan clenched his teeth tight together and let the dummy answer. "Ny name," it warbled, "is Gryan Grain."

Icky and Stinky howled with laughter. "Gonk!" cried Icky. "Say it again, Bryan!"

"Ny name," repeated Bryan, "is Gryan Grain."

Icky and Stinky laughed fit to bust, and a great swell of satisfaction rose within Bryan. Normally he couldn't make people laugh to save his life.

**Note from Blue Soup**
True fans of the House of Fun will know that, in a past adventure, Bryan really did have to make

someone laugh to save his life. Obviously he succeeded, but only by resorting to animal noises, a wonky-legged loony dance, and several other idiotic activities he would never want his children to see.

If you know who forced Bryan to be funny, write your answer on a postcard, address it to The Generations to Come, place it in a time capsule and bury it beneath the foundations of an important new public building. One day people of the future will discover how clever you are, but it won't make you as bigheaded as Bryan.

"Right," said Bryan. "You wait here, and don't go anywhere, and when I say, come upstairs to the landing outside the Dressing-up Room, where two chairs will be waiting for you."

So saying, Bryan hurried up the stairs with his new pal tucked under his arm. Twenty minutes passed, during which Icky got very fidgety and Stinky got rather fudgety due to a forgotten toffee he discovered behind his left ear.

"You can come up now!" yelled Bryan, at last.

Icky tore up the stairs like a ferret in fear of its

life. Stinky ambled comfortably behind. They found the two promised chairs at the side of the landing facing the doorway to the Dressing-up Room, which had been covered by a makeshift pair of curtains hanging off a bungee strap. Suddenly the curtains were ripped apart to reveal the bizarre spectacle of Bryan and Gryan, now dressed in identical dinner jackets and bow ties.

"Hello, good day, and top of the morning to you!" cried Bryan, even though it was now evening.

"*I need a doctor,*" squeaked Gryan.

"You need a doctor, Gryan?" replied Bryan. "Why is that?"

"*I've got a strawgerry growing out of my gum,*" peeped Gryan.

"You want to put some cream on that!" replied Bryan.

Bryan paused, waiting for the laugh, which never came, as Stinky didn't get the joke and Icky was feeling a little bit scared. Undaunted, Bryan pressed on with the act.

"Gryan!" he cried. "What's the difference between roast beef and pea soup?"

"*Anyone can roast geef!*" squealed Gryan.

That one passed Stinky by as well, while Icky was getting more and more obsessed by the fact that Bryan and Gryan had identical moles on their right cheeks. Had Bryan always had that mole or was he wearing make-up to look like Gryan? Or was it Gryan who was wearing the make-up to look like Bryan?

Either way, Bryan was not the least put off by the awful silence coming from the audience. He continued with the routine for a full half hour, including drinking a glass of squash while Gryan sang "All Things Gright and Geautiful" and nearly choking in the process, which did at least raise a chuckle from Icky and Stinky. Bryan and Gryan completed their act with a bow, then announced there was a special Meet The Stars event to follow, in which the audience got the chance to speak to Bryan and Gryan in the flesh, or the wood in Gryan's case.

"Are there any questions you'd like to ask me?" enquired Bryan.

"Yes," replied Icky. "Bryan, why do you think you're funny?"

Bryan's face turned frosty. "Just because you

don't get my sense of humour," he snapped.

"But Bryan," said Icky, "no one gets your sense of humour."

"I can tell you one person who does!" rasped Bryan.

"Who's that, Bryan?" asked Icky.

"*This* person," replied Bryan, patting Gryan lovingly on the shoulder.

"Bryan," said Stinky. "It's only a doll."

Bryan's hands clamped round Gryan's ears. "Don't listen to him, Gryan," he urged. "He's only jealous."

## Chapter Four

That night Bryan made a little bed for Gryan next to his own, and the two of them could be heard chatting amiably long into the night. Gryan was the perfect listener, never interrupting, nodding in all the right places, and showing such genuine interest in Bryan's general knowledge of general knowledge generally.

Next morning Bryan sprang down to breakfast full of the joys of life. He had been making plans, and as usual, it was Icky and Stinky's job to fit in with them.

"We're going to put on a show," he pronounced.

"'We'?" repeated Stinky. "Who's 'we'?"

"Gryan and I will be the main act, of course," said Bryan. "You and Icky will be the supporting bill."

Stinky didn't like the sound of this at all. He remembered bills from the old days. They were things which arrived in the post and made his mum and dad argue.

Icky didn't like the sound of it either. The only bill he knew was stuck on the front of a duck's face. He didn't fancy having one and he certainly didn't fancy supporting Bryan on it if he did.

Fortunately, however, Bryan explained in a little more detail. They were simply going to put on a fantastic show, starring the Amazing Gryan Grain, also featuring the Slightly Talented Icky and Stinky, who would be performing ... well, whatever they felt like performing, other than a ventriloquist act.

"But I'm no good at anything," complained Stinky.

"You'll think of something," Bryan assured him.

"Like what?" asked Icky.

"I don't know ... a flea circus!" replied Bryan, impatiently.

"I haven't got any fleas," moaned Stinky. "The maggots have eaten them."

"Well, you'll just have to play the spoons,"

snapped Bryan. "You've got to do something, because it's on the posters."

"The what?" asked Icky.

Bryan drew a rolled-up sheet of paper from his pocket and smoothed it out:

## ROLL UP! ROLL UP!

### FOR THE GREATEST SHOW ON EARTH

#### STARRING

# THE AMAZING
# GRYAN GRAIN

### ALSO FEATURING ICKY AND STINKY

### HOUSE OF FUN
### SATURDAY 1 MAY 7.30 P.M.

## HURRY! NEARLY SOLD OUT!

"Hmm," said Icky. "And how many of these posters have you made?"

"Just the five hundred so far," replied Bryan. "I don't think we need to put up too many, because we've also got the door-to-door leaflets, and the stickers for people to swap, and the giant spoonbeam message in the sky."

Greatest show on earth? Giant spoonbeam message? Bryan really had lost it this time. His plans were so crazy that only a reckless mentalist would go along with them.

"When do we get started?" asked Icky.

# Chapter Five

The three housemates gazed up at Lord Bastien's Hump, the highest hill in the county, straining their eyes to see the spoonbeam projector at the summit. No one ever went near that projector, which was protected by a Vardanite force field, and operated by remote control from space by the Spoonheads.

"We must establish a Base Camp," declared Bryan.

"A base camp?" repeated Icky. "Why do we need a base camp?"

"All mountaineers establish base camps," replied Bryan.

"It's only a hill!" said Icky.

As usual, however, Bryan insisted they do

everything properly. Not only were they to establish a base camp, they were also to be roped together and kitted out with snow-goggles and a week's supply of Kendal mint cake.

As it turned out, they only had a large plastic bag for a base camp anyway. Bryan converted this into a makeshift tent with a large stick as a pole, then left a diary inside it for the benefit of future generations. Icky took up position at the front of the climbing party, as he was the most impatient, with Stinky second and Bryan bringing up the rear. Bryan secretly thought this was the safest place to be, until he had a worrying thought.

"Stinky," he asked. "What did you have for breakfast this morning?"

"An omelette," replied Stinky.

"Ah," said Bryan. "That's all right then."

"With baked beans, Brussels sprouts and bran flakes," added Stinky.

Bryan's knees weakened. An awful memory came back to him, the memory of being the back end of a panto horse, when Stinky was the front end, and …

… it really was a terrible memory.

"I'll go second," declared Bryan. "You go behind me."

"OK," said Stinky, who, as usual, had no idea what Bryan was thinking.

The three housemates set off up the hill, which, in truth, was not that steep and not at all dangerous. Soon they were enjoying fantastic views over town and country, as far as Dragon's Cove, where the *SS Entertainer* still lay beached.

It really was quite a pleasant stroll, even when tied together with a rope in heavy anoraks and snow-goggles.

All good things come to an end, however, and on Lord Bastien's Hump that end was the Vardanite force field. The force field stretched like a hazy blue belt right round the hill, with no way under, over or through. Bryan had had a theory they could dig a tunnel beneath it, but the hill at this point was almost solid rock.

It was at this point that Stinky made a brave suggestion. As you may know, Stinky quite liked force fields, which for some reason gave him a pleasant tingly sensation rather than blasting him backwards like a knockout blow from a giant electric boxer. Maybe, he suggested, he could lean on the force field and the others could climb over him.

"Careful, Stinky," said Icky, freeing his great pal from the climbing-rope. "You've never tried it with a Vardanite force field."

Stinky paused for a moment. "What's the worst that could happen?" he asked.

"You could end up as a pile of smouldering dust," replied Icky.

Stinky decided to try just one finger, and if that ended up as smouldering dust, not to bother with anything else. Approaching the shimmering blue line, he slowly raised his right arm, forgetting that Bryan had told him never to raise an arm until he'd either washed or used a good deodorant. Almost immediately a strange change came over the force field, which turned from blue to a pale sickly green, then began breaking out in holes, which grew larger and larger, till they joined together and weren't holes any more because there was nothing for them to be holes in. Apart from a few stray buzzing tussocks of grass, the force field was no more.

"Stinky!" cried Icky. "Your armpit's disabled the force field!"

Stinky turned to the housemates and was about to raise an arm in triumph when Bryan's fearful cry prevented him from disabling them as well.

"To the summit!" cried Icky, but just as he sprang forward, he caught sight of something Very Disturbing Indeed. "Eurrgh!" he cried.

"What is it?" asked Stinky.

"Slugs!" cried Icky.

"*Slugs?*" sneered Bryan. "Who's afraid of—"

The voice died in Bryan's throat, to be quickly followed by a whimpering noise, a bit like a baby makes before it bursts into tears. His gaze had fallen on the slugs in question, which were typically ugly and slimy, but also four foot long. They were dotted randomly around the top of the hill, a bit like sheep or cows, quietly grazing. Behind each one was a wide trail of glistening slime.

"Wow," said Icky. "Maybe the force field turned them that big."

"Do slugs eat people?" asked Stinky.

"Let's ask them," suggested Icky.

"Can they speak?" asked Stinky.

"They're *molluscs*," scoffed Bryan. "Everyone knows the Spoonheads didn't teach *molluscs* to speak."

Almost as if it heard, the nearest slug turned its head towards Bryan. It really was a grotesque head, covered in blotches and veins, with two long tentacles ending in swollen milky eyes.

Bryan began to shake gently. "My premonition…" he mumbled.

"Prem-a-what?" said Stinky.

"Someone's going to die," muttered Bryan.

"Rubbish," said Icky. "We'll just keep our distance from them and we'll be fine."

Icky pressed on, and as he'd re-attached the climbing-rope, so did Bryan and Stinky. The projector was not far away now, but they couldn't take a straight path there owing to the slugs, which seemed to get more numerous by the second. Some were glassy-smooth and pale, some rough and red, some covered in leopard spots, some in tiny yellow dots. For the most part, however, they didn't seem that interested in the housemates, but if they *were* to turn nasty … it didn't bear thinking about.

At last, by the wiggliest route imaginable, the housemates reached the summit. There stood the spoon-beam projector, in all its glory, a super-tech cannon of light programmed to fill the sky the moment the sun went down.

**Note from Blue Soup**

You may be wondering what messages were projected by the Spoonheads. Keep wondering.

Bryan dug into his pocket and produced a small square of wundaphane on which his advert was written. He had studied the workings of the spoonbeam projector and knew that there was a small slot on one side, into which such a message could be inserted. That message would then override any others for at least fifteen minutes.

Only one problem. Bryan could not find the small slot anywhere.

"Must be on the other side," he mused.

The three housemates took hold of the projector, which was mounted on a rotating stand, and with a huge effort swung it round. As the other side appeared, however, so did the most humungous black slug, which clung to the side of the projector like a great bulbous lozenge.

"We-urrrrrrgh!" cried Bryan, backing away in horror.

"That's scary," said Stinky.

"We'll have to get it off," said Icky.

"G-get it off?" stammered Bryan. "H-how do you propose to do that?"

"Maybe you could tempt it away with a nice leaf," suggested Icky.

"No way!" said Bryan. "What if it prefers me to the leaf?"

"Maybe we could hit it with something," suggested Stinky.

"Such as?" asked Icky.

"A stick," replied Stinky. "Look, there's some over there."

Sure enough, there was the remains of a rowing boat nearby with three shabby oars inside it. It had probably been carried up there in the old days by some drunken students. Icky fetched the oars and tested one for strength. "Are we trying to hurt it, or kill it?" he asked.

"Just trying to make it move," replied Stinky, who didn't much like the idea of hurting anything, even less killing it.

"But if we don't kill it," said Icky, "it might turn vicious."

Bryan gave an impatient sigh. "Why don't you

simply get the oars under it, use them as levers, and prise it off?" he suggested.

"OK," said Icky. "Let's do that." He handed one oar to Stinky, and tried to hand the other to Bryan, who was having none of it.

"I'm allergic," he claimed.

"What, to oars, or slugs?" asked Icky.

"Both," replied Bryan.

"Come on, Stinky," said Icky. "We'll do it."

With that, Icky approached the giant slug, followed nervously by Stinky, while Bryan retreated to a slightly safe distance, then a safe distance, then a very safe distance indeed.

"I'll work an oar under the head end," said Icky, "and you work an oar under the ... other end."

The two housemates got to work. It wasn't easy. The slug was stuck fast to the projector with slobbery mucus, and as they disturbed it, even more slime came bubbling out. Bit by bit, however, they forced their oars under its great blubbery body, till only half the oars were showing. These were balanced on the projector, with the ends hanging over the edge. With sufficient force on these ends, the great beast would surely be levered away.

"When I say," said Icky, "push with everything you've got."

"Got you," replied Stinky.

"One ... two ... THREE!" cried Icky.

Icky and Stinky walloped the oars like a pair of charging rhinos. There was an almighty GLOOP, and next moment the slug was flying through the air as if it had been fired from a catapult. Hardly able to believe their success, the two housemates high-fived, whooped and hollered in triumph.

"See that, Bryan!?" cried Icky. "See that, Bryan!?"

There was no reply.

"He missed it!" moaned Stinky.

"He's run away!" scoffed Icky.

Suddenly there was a muffled groan. It came from roughly where the slug had landed.

"That sounded like Bryan," said Icky.

Stinky surveyed the scene. "Icky" he asked, "was the slug wearing shoes?"

"Definitely not" replied Icky.

"In that case," said Stinky, "I think Bryan's legs are underneath it."

Icky followed Stinky's gaze. Sure enough, a thin pair of legs could be seen poking out beneath the monster slug, wearing sensible shoes that could only be Bryan's.

"Wow," said Icky. "That was bad luck."

"I suppose we'd better get him out," said Stinky.

Part of Icky thought Bryan deserved to be stuck under the slug, perhaps forever, but he gamely picked up his oar and followed Stinky over to their stricken housemate. Together they began levering the great mollusc again, except this time the slug was twice as hard to move, and spewed out twice as much slime. With a heroic heave, however, they finally turned the monster over, to reveal Bryan flat on his back, covered from top to toe in foul yellow gunk. Stinky, who wasn't too bothered about gunk himself, pulled Bryan to a sitting position and wiped the slime off his face with his sleeve.

"I want my mu—" blathered Bryan. "I want my mu— my mu— my malted milk biscuits!"

# Chapter Six

Bryan's terrible experience was not in vain. That evening, as the sun went down, the three house-mates sat on the roof of the House of Fun, and to their delight, saw THE GREATEST SHOW ON EARTH come up across the sky. Their advert looked frabjous, apart from Gryan's name, which looked more like Gryan Groan on account of the slug slime smeared over the wundaphane.

"We're famous!" cried Icky.

"Now everyone will come to our show!" declared Bryan.

"Will we get in trouble?" wondered Stinky.

Icky and Bryan refused to be brought down by such an idea. "The Spoonbeams will love it," declared Icky.

"They'll think, 'what cheeky monkeys did this?'," added Bryan.

"They'll laugh their socks off," said Icky.

"They'll invite us to do another one," suggested Bryan.

Stinky wanted to be convinced, but all this talk of monkeys and socks was making him uneasy. He didn't know much about Spoonheads but was fairly sure they had no sense of humour and absolutely sure they had no feet.

It was not long before the housemates discovered what the Spoonheads did think of their jolly jape. Next morning, there was a black envelope lying on the front door mat. It was an envelope with a window in it, and in the window were the words **TO THE RESIDENTS OF THE HOUSE OF FUN** in serious capital letters.

"I don't like the look of this," said Stinky.

"Probably a request for tickets," said Bryan, but he didn't sound convincing.

Icky tore open the envelope, unfolded the letter inside, and began reading it out loud:

# TO THE RESIDENTS OF THE HOUSE OF FUN

Hi guys!

The Spoonheads General Council has noted that an unauthorised spoonbeam message was projected yesterday. That message appears to have come from you.

Humans are welcome to project messages, but only through the usual channels, which you have chosen to ignore.

We are, as a result, very annoyed.

Mad even.

We have therefore decided on the following course of action.

A Spoonbot will be in attendance at the performance you have advertised. If your advertisement is found to be untrue in any way (if, for example, it is not actually "the greatest show on earth"), you will be removed from your place of residence forthwith and exhibited alongside the old humans in the Upper Whipsnip Space Zoo.

The Spoonbot's judgement will be final and there is no appeal against this procedure.

Sorry, guys!

Your friend,

## Glun Portastig 5

Secretary, Spoonheads General Council

The housemates were gobsmacked. Any letter with the word "forthwith" in it had to be taken seriously.

"This is your fault, Bryan!" cried Icky.

"You made me do it!" cried Bryan.

"I don't want to go to the space zoo!" cried Stinky.

All three began pacing this way and that at frantic speed, gabbling furiously without anyone listening to anyone else. After a few minutes of this they wound up in a circle of deafening babble, mouths opening and closing meaninglessly, until eventually fatigue took its toll and one by one they fell into a sorry silence.

"OK," said Icky, rather more calmly. "Let's think of something positive to say."

"We're all going to die," murmured Bryan.

"I said be positive," said Icky.

"I'm positive we're all going to die," replied Bryan.

"I've got an idea," announced Stinky.

"Is it a good idea?" asked Icky.

"Um ..." said Stinky.

"Never mind, Stinky," said Icky, patting his great mate on the shoulder. "Let's hear it anyway."

"Well," said Stinky. "What if we *do* put on the greatest show on Earth?"

"But Stinky," said Icky. "Bryan's not funny and we haven't even got an act."

"I could saw you in half," suggested Stinky.

Icky viewed Stinky quizzically. He was used to his great mate making bizarre suggestions, but this one really took the biscuit. "Any idea how you're going to do that?" he asked.

"Not really," replied Stinky. "But I did see a magician do it once."

"Hmm," said Icky. "I don't want to say I'm against it, Stinky, but if you *are* going to saw me in half, I would prefer it if you know what you're doing."

"OK," replied Stinky. "I'll do a wordsearch."

"Wordsearch?" repeated Icky.

"Is that the word, when you find out about things?" asked Stinky.

"Research?" suggested Icky.

"Research," repeated Stinky. "That's the one."

Stinky smiled broadly, Icky looked no less worried, and Bryan frowned darkly. "What do you mean I'm not funny?" he growled.

"You're going to need some better jokes," said Icky.

"Ha!" said Bryan. "We'll see what Gryan says about that!"

Stinky's heart sank. Maybe it was wiser just to pack their cases for the space zoo now.

# Chapter Seven

Nothing was seen of Bryan for the next twenty-four hours. Stinky did hear him in the bathroom, running a sinky-bath for Gryan, while Icky caught him singing Gryan a warbly lullaby at bedtime, but the housemates took care not to disturb him. The longer Bryan spent with Gryan, hopefully, the better their act would become.

Stinky, meanwhile, was determined not to let Icky down. He set off into town, not really knowing where he was going, but confident he would find somebody who knew more about magic tricks than he did. After all, everybody knew more than Stinky about magic tricks, or about anything really.

Town had changed a lot since the Spoonheads closed down all the shops and melted down the tills. There was a wild variety of places and spaces, catering for every interest under the sun. The Museum of Skateboards stood opposite the Random Tattoo Centre; the Non-stop Bouncing Arcade shared a front door with the Experimental Sweet-boiling Club. It was all a bit of a mystery to Stinky, due to his problems with words of more than four letters, but eventually he arrived at a tall, thin ancient structure with a mystic air about it. Sure enough, through the window he could see boys and girls waving strange wands around. It certainly looked worth a try.

Stinky walked in. He was immediately confronted by a blonde girl in a top hat and tails, who produced a bunch of flowers from nowhere with a great flourish.

"Welcome," she said, "to the White Rabbit Conjuring Club."

"Hi," replied Stinky. "Does anyone know about magic here?"

"It is the White Rabbit Conjuring Club," repeated the girl.

"Right," replied Stinky. "Does anyone know about magic here?"

The girl frowned. "What do you need to know?" she asked.

"How to saw someone in half," replied Stinky.

"I'll get the Great Wangadanga," announced the girl.

Stinky soon found himself sitting opposite an odd-looking boy, with a suspiciously fake-looking tan, long waxy fingers and hair so slick it could have been made in a mould.

"What you are proposing is very dangerous," he declared, "in the wrong hands."

Stinky studied his own hands. The right one was on the right and the left one was on the left, or so Icky had told him, so with any luck they weren't wrong.

"Listen very carefully," whispered the Great Wangadanga, "and forget nothing."

Stinky nodded, but was already feeling worried.

"The key to the trick is in the box," began the Great Wangadanga. "This must be craftily designed to seem smaller than it really is. Your assistant then gets into the box and appears to put their feet through the end. However, these feet are actually fakes, which you move by means of an invisible thread. The assistant, who must be very flexible, then pulls their knees up to their chin and turns their body sideways. You then pretend to cut them in half and wheel the two halves apart, before rejoining them and, hey presto, putting your assistant back together again."

Stinky nodded again. "Would you mind repeating that," he asked, "about ten times?"

Wearily, the Great Wangadanga repeated it once, while Stinky fought with all his might to cram it into his brain like a great pile of socks into a rickety chest of drawers.

"And where will I find the special box?" asked Stinky.

"You can have my old one," replied the Great Wangadanga, "but what will you give me for it?"

"I can give you a ticket to the Greatest Show on Earth," replied Stinky.

"That sounds a good deal," replied the Great Wangadanga.

For a moment Stinky felt guilty, then he remembered that their performance really was going to be the Greatest Show on Earth, so maybe it was a good deal after all.

The Great Wangadanga fetched Stinky the special box, which reminded Stinky of the box they'd put his great grandma in. Vaguely he wondered if that was also part of a magic trick, except magic tricks didn't normally make everybody cry.

"The feet are inside," declared the Great Wangadanga.

"And the key?" asked Stinky.

"The key?" repeated the Great Wangadanga.

"You said the key was in the box," said Stinky.

The Great Wangadanga viewed Stinky quizzically. "Are you sure you know what you're doing?" he asked.

"Could you just repeat the instructions again?" asked Stinky.

Stinky really did try his best to remember the instructions on the way home. It wasn't easy, especially while he was pushing an old supermarket trolley full of magic box. Every now and then a couple of words would fall off, or find themselves in the wrong sentence, and sometimes whole sentences would rearrange themselves in a different order. Even so, Stinky was determined to remember just enough to be able to guess the rest.

Just as Stinky was on the final stretch home, however, he heard a familiar voice, or rather, two familiar voices. One was a ponderous, know-all, twit kind of voice, and the other a high-pitched slightly pathetic reply. Sure enough, they were the voices of Bryan and Gryan, sitting at the edge of Cormorant Lake, watching the sunset. They had their backs to Stinky, so he was able to park his trolley and creep close enough to eavesdrop.

Stinky was really hoping to hear Bryan and Gryan practising their hilarious routine. But it was not that kind of a conversation.

"Don't you find," mused Bryan, "the more one looks at beauty, the more one is aware of tragedy?"

*"Life is so very grief,"* peeped Gryan.

"Indeed," replied Bryan, solemnly, "and our great deeds are merely castles of sand, which the tide of time will surely sweep away."

There was a short silence.

*"I don't think I'll gother gracticing any more,"* peeped Gryan.

"That's another matter," said Bryan.

*"There's no goint,"* peeped Gryan.

"That's enough of that talk!" snapped Bryan. "You will do as I say!"

*"Why have I always got to do what you say?"* pleaded Gryan.

"Because I say so!" barked Bryan.

"*It's not fair!*" bleated Gryan.

"Life isn't fair!" snapped Bryan.

Stinky had heard enough. The argument was reminding him of the rows he'd had with his parents before they were sucked into the space zoo. Since his parents had gone, Stinky had almost forgotten that life wasn't fair, mainly because generally life *was* fair, now they'd got rid of the people who said it wasn't.

Needless to say, Icky was well impressed by Stinky's magic box. "Frabjous!" he cried. "When shall we start?"

"It is getting late," Stinky pointed out, "and I'm very tired."

"We'd better start now then," said Icky, "or you'll never get to bed."

Before Stinky could protest, Icky had pulled the box apart and discovered the false feet inside. "What are these for?" he asked.

In that terrible moment, Stinky realised that all the remaining instructions had drained out of his head. Eavesdropping on Bryan had been a costly mistake.

"They're spares," he mumbled.

"What, in case you cut my feet off?" asked Icky.

"Er …" muttered Stinky.

"These feet are pink!" protested Icky. "My feet are brown!"

"Let's chuck them," suggested Stinky.

Icky did just that. "What we do need," he declared, "is a saw."

"A saw," repeated Stinky, desperately trying to remember the bit of instruction which mentioned saws.

"We'd better get one," said Icky.

"OK," replied Stinky.

The housemates knew that there was a huge assortment of tools, nails, widgets and gadgets in the Time-Travel Garage, but had never actually investigated these. That was because every time they went to find a tool, nail, widget or gadget, Icky got distracted by the Time-Travel van and insisted they took a trip there and then to a place where and when.

Stinky was taking no chances this time. He went up to the Dressing-up Room, found the panto blinkers which went with the panto horse costume, and carefully fitted them on to Icky. As they entered the Time-Travel Garage he focussed his great mate on the far end of the room, where the tools were stored, and kept Icky's line of vision well away from his favourite vehicle.

Icky soon discovered that the tools, nails, widgets and gadgets were almost as interesting as the famous van. Stinky's Uncle Nero, who (as everyone knows) built the House of Fun, was a very methodical person (look it up) and had stored every single screw, rivet, G-clamp and camping mallet in a carefully labelled box or on an equally meticulous hook. It was like looking at the most frabjous hardware store in the universe, with rows of shelves stretching up into the heavens, and in the midst of it all, a line of saws of every size and shape imaginable.

The two housemates studied the saws, and their labels, considering which would be best suited to cutting somebody in half.

"What's a fretsaw?" asked Stinky.

"A saw that worries," replied Icky, who liked to know the answers, even when he didn't.

"What would a saw worry about?" asked Stinky.

"Bad teeth," replied Icky.

"How about a mitre saw?" asked Stinky.

"That's for cutting hats off bishops' heads," replied Icky.

"Is that necessary?" asked Stinky.

"Sometimes," replied Icky, "when they get big-headed."

"A two-man saw!" exclaimed Stinky. "That would do, cos there's two of us!"

"Except one of us is in a box," Icky pointed out.

"Oh yes," replied Stinky. "I forgot that."

"Hmm," said Icky. "A carcass saw. That might do the trick."

"What's a carcass?" asked Stinky.

"A lump of dead meat," replied Icky.

"Perfect," said Stinky.

"Except I won't be dead," Icky pointed out.

"And the saw won't be going into you," added Stinky.

"In which case," said Icky, "we might as well choose any saw."

"Good point," replied Stinky.

With that, the two housemates selected a big

shiny butcher's meat-splitting saw and set off towards the magic box.

As soon as Icky and Stinky reached the hall, however, they realised that something was badly wrong. At the front door were a few meagre possessions wrapped in a spotted hankie, tied to the end of a stick, balanced on Bryan's shoulder.

"I've had an argument," declared Bryan.

"With a dummy?" asked Stinky.

"I may be back," replied Bryan. "I may not. Who knows."

"You can't leave!" cried Icky.

"Don't you start," said Bryan. "I've had enough with Gryan telling me what to do."

With that, Bryan dramatically flung open the door, and was gone.

"He'll be back," declared Icky.

"How do you know?" asked Stinky.

"He always is," replied Icky.

"That's true," agreed Stinky.

"Let's get on with the magic trick," said Icky.

"OK," said Stinky.

The great mates made their way back to the magic box and, without further ado, Icky climbed inside, making sure his feet went through the two holes which had been conveniently cut at one end.

"Are you sure I'm not supposed to do something, like tuck up into a very small ball?" asked Icky.

A dim tiny memory came back to Stinky, like the glimmer of a dying torch in a dark cave. Something about knees ... chins ... hey presto ...

Just as quickly, the tiny light faded.

"Just lie still and the magic will happen," said Stinky, "I think."

Stinky inserted the saw into the slot in the middle of the box and began steadily moving it back and forth. At first the saw moved quite easily and smoothly ... then things became a little more stodgy and Stinky had to put all his weight behind the saw to keep it moving. Meanwhile Icky had become aware of a pain in his side, quite a sharp pain actually, but ever since Icky had done karate he had prided himself in keeping a stiff upper lip and blocking out everything from minor discomfort to outright agony. So he lay still, imagined he was being tortured for a vital secret, and made not a whimper, while Stinky forced the saw back and forth with all the might he could muster.

It was at this point that Stinky became aware of something dripping on to his foot.

"Icky," said Stinky, "there's stuff coming out of the box."

"What kind of stuff?" asked Icky.

"Red stuff," replied Stinky.

"Ah," said Icky. "That'll be blood."

"What?" cried Stinky, alarmed. "Your blood?"

"I guess so," replied Icky. "Would you do us a favour, Stinks, and stop sawing?"

Stinky, who wasn't aware that he was still sawing, stopped instantly, and at this point realised that the red stuff was also generously spread across the saw blade.

"S-something's gone wrong," he stammered.

"Guess the box wasn't very magic," replied Icky.

Stinky hurriedly freed Icky from the unmagic box, to discover a horrible and dramatic gash on his great mate's side.

"Sorry, Icky!" he cried.

"Wow," said Icky. "I look like something out of a horror movie."

"Shall I get you a plaster?" asked Stinky.

"You'd better disinfect the wound first," replied Icky.

"Disaffect the wound?" gabbled Stinky. "How do I do that?"

"Go up to the medical cabinet," replied Icky, "and fetch the Surgical Spirit."

"Surgical spirit?" said Stinky. "Is that some kind of genie?"

"No, Stinky," replied Icky. "It's a clear liquid in a glass bottle, and it starts with a sss."

"Got it," said Stinky.

Stinky hurried up to the Undersea World of Uncle Nero Bathroom, where the medicine cabinet lived. Unfortunately, however, during a particularly boring week, the housemates had had a medicine fight, and pills, bandages and bottles were still strewn everywhere.

Stinky scrabbled wildly through the mess, until to his great relief he spotted a bottle which fitted the description Icky had given. With difficulty, because Stinky was not a great reader, he began to read the label:

**SULPHURIC ACID**

**EXTRA STRONG**

WARNING: HANDLE WITH EXTREME CARE. DO NOT SWALLOW OR ALLOW CONTACT WITH SKIN. IN CASE OF ACCIDENTS IMMEDIATELY SEEK MEDICAL ADVICE.

"Hmm," said Stinky. "Starts with a sss. Must be the one."

Stinky sped back downstairs with the bottle. He felt terrible about what he'd done to Icky, but it was a comfort to know that he was about to make things so much better.

"Found it, Icks!" he cried, triumphantly brandishing the bottle.

"Well done, Stinks," replied Icky. "Now just pour it all over the wound, and don't worry if I cry out, because it does tend to sting."

"Don't worry if I cry out," repeated Stinky to himself, "because it does tend to sting." He pulled the stopper out of the bottle, lined it up over Icky's injured side, and prepared to pour. "Brace yourself, Icks," he said.

"Ready for anything, Stinks," replied Icky.

"Three ..." began Stinky.

"Two ..."

"One ..."

# ARRRRRRRRRRRGH!

"Are you all right, Stinky?" asked Icky, surprised to see his great mate doubled up in pain.

"Just some cramp in my leg," replied Stinky, straightening up again, and fortunately keeping the bottle balanced upright.

"Tell you what," said Icky, "let's just test that surgical spirit. My uncle Naz said never use old medicines till you've tried them out on the cat."

"We haven't got a cat," replied Stinky.

"We'll test it on Gryan." suggested Icky.

"Good idea," replied Stinky.

Stinky fetched Gryan, who had nothing much to say in Bryan's absence. He propped the dumb dummy against the wall, where he sat limply, mouth hanging open and eyes staring into the middle distance.

"I'll just pour a bit on his foot," declared Stinky.

Stinky did just that. Immediately a foul odour filled the room and a thick cloud of acrid brown smoke arose from Gryan's foot, or what used to be his foot, as his appendage was rotting away in the most dramatic fashion. Soon there was nothing left but a stump, smoking gently like a snuffed candle.

"Hmm," said Stinky.

"Hmm," said Icky.

"Do you still want me to use it on you?" asked Stinky.

"I don't think so," replied Icky.

"Bryan'll go mad," said Stinky.

"Maybe we can get Gryan a boot," suggested Icky.

"I'd better hide him for now," said Stinky. He duly removed the stricken dummy, returning five minutes later satisfied that he'd found a Very Clever Hiding Place Which Bryan Would Never Find. Icky did consider asking exactly where this was, but he was feeling quite weak from the loss of blood.

"Maybe we should get a doctor," he suggested.

There was only one problem with this idea. There weren't any doctors left, not on Earth anyway.

Like everything else, they had been replaced by Blue Soup, except even Blue Soup had surgery hours, and it was now past bedtime for all sensible people.

Just then, however, Icky remembered a flyer which had come under the back door a few weeks before. It was always worth reading flyers which came this way, since (as you all know), beyond the back door was nothing but outer space.

Icky found the flyer and studied it again:

**FOR ALL MEDICAL EMERGENCIES
VISIT DR LOVETHANG'S MOBILE SPACE CLINIC
THE CLINIC WILL BE IN YOUR SECTOR OF
THE INFINITE COSMOS ON**
*Tuesdays and Thursdays*

"It's Tuesday," said Icky. "Let's go."

"Let's go" was one of Icky's favourite phrases, and one which Stinky could never resist. Stinky grabbed a tea-towel, applied a temporary dressing to Icky's wound and dragged out the space-module-dishwasher-thing which needed a good dusting and a new battery, but was otherwise ready for action.

76

"Let's hope that mysterious problem is cured and the launch doesn't go horribly wrong again," said Stinky.

"We'll soon find out," replied Icky.


## Note from Blue Soup

Sorry to butt in here, but a certain reader who will be nameless (Giles Brenda Fremling of 9, Radio Rd, Chipping Sodbury) writes to me whenever he/she spots a mistake in a Stinky Finger story, and will undoubtedly have noticed that the space module featured on page 82 of Crazy Party at the House of Fun only carries one person. Well, Giles, you can save yourself the postage this time, because I upgrade all space-module-dishwasher-things every year, just as people in the Old Days used to upgrade their mobile phones. I now return you to our story.


## Note from Blue Soup

Sorry again. We must have missed the launch while I was telling you about Giles Brenda Fremling. The housemates are now speeding through space at 3 billion ultralight years a second.

# Chapter Eight

Luckily the Batnav was working perfectly. One of the improvements in the new space module was the use of a leaf-nosed bat to send out sonar across the heavens in order to locate solid bodies such as moons and mobile health clinics. Like most animals which had come into contact with the Spoonheads it could also speak, but this was unfortunately in such high-pitched squeaks that the housemates could not detect them. As a result there were many embarrassing conversations on the way to the space clinic, with the bat getting very excited about its funny stories and the housemates laughing gaily when the bat seemed to have reached the punchline.

This worked reasonably well until the bat told

Icky and Stinky about the death of its mother, after which all conversation ground to a halt.

Eventually they came in sight of a bizarre craft, shaped exactly like a bog brush of the Days of Old. A huge towery-masty thing sat atop a great white cylinder surrounded in spikes, with spacecrafts of all natures docked around it. From the way these craft flew in and out it was obvious they were driven by sick things. The housemates had surely found Dr Lovethang's space clinic.

With the help of Batnav, the space module parked up and Icky and Stinky made their way down the nearest connector to the main corridor. Here they were surprised to find all manner of beggars, most ill or injured and some playing peculiar musical instruments. These, however, were nothing compared with the sight which greeted Icky and Stinky in the Waiting Womb. This giant chamber was stocked with every creature imaginable, all watched over by a team of galactic bouncers which really did bounce, as they were completely round, apart from a thick neck on the top of their bodies, circled by a bow-tie which doubled as a ticket machine.

Icky and Stinky took a ticket and seated themselves next to something vaguely human, apart from the fact it was completely transparent and had some kind of mechanical dicky-bird trapped in its gullet. Next to this oddity were three purply aliens, all skewered together on a spike of moonrock, a bit like a kebab or the midfield of a table footy team. Opposite, meanwhile, was a wobbly jelly thing covered from head to feet by little red toadstools, doing its best to cover a coughing mouth with one of its many hands.

Icky did his best not to stare at this sickly creature, but Icky was not very good at not staring when something really interested him, and after a while the wobbly jelly thing began to look quite annoyed. However, just as it was about to get up and ask Icky what he was staring at (or whatever wobbly jelly things say in this situation), a frail little stick-insect-type thing asked it a question. Before it had time to put one of its hands over its mouth, the wobbly jelly thing had coughed right in the stick-insect-type thing's face.

In an instant, the frail creature's head was also covered in little red toadstools, which then spread like a sheet of flame all over its body. With a faint unearthly cry it dropped to the ground, shrivelled up like a salted slug, and was hastily whipped out of the room by the nearest bouncers.

"Wow," said Stinky.

"That's scary," said Icky.

The transparent humanoid leaned close to the two housemates. "The grotula," it croaked.

"I thought so," replied Icky, who'd never heard of the grotula in his life.

"There is no cure for the grotula," croaked the transparent humanoid. He gave a weak sigh and a shudder, and the dicky-bird in his gullet chirruped as if in agreement.

Icky's number could not come up too soon, and when it did he made sure to give the wobbly jelly thing a wide berth. It really was a bad idea, in Icky's opinion, to put all these sick things in a doctor's clinic, especially ones with the grotula.

Dr Lovethang's door opened with a quiet hum and Icky walked in. Dr Lovethang sat in the centre of the room behind his desk, very much like a normal doctor, except this one had eight huge octopus arms, all busy on different tasks, and a great swollen glob of a head into which at least fifty eyes were randomly planted. Behind him, on the other side of a glassy partition, an army of baby aliens bounced furiously. Each had a rainbow tube connected to it, so that it was pretty obvious to any intelligent lifeform that this was how the space clinic got its power.

"Whassup?" said Icky.

One of Dr Lovethang's arms worked quickly on a voice decoder until Icky's language was recognised.

"Take. A. Seat." said the doctor, in a surprisingly high and rather nasal voice.

Icky sat on the chair beside Dr Lovethang's desk.

"What. Seems. To. Be. The. Problem?" asked the doctor.

"I've got a gash," replied Icky. "On my side."

"Pop. Up. On. The. Couch." ordered Dr Lovethang, "And. Pop. Your. Top. Off."

Icky did as requested. Most of the doctor's eyes then detached themselves from his face and roved all over Icky's body, finally congregating in a bubbling huddle round the wound.

"This. Wound. Requires. Neutralisation. And. Tissue. Repair." declared Dr Lovethang.

"Can you do it?" asked Icky.

"Certainly." replied the doctor. "That. Will. Be. 25 million. UK Earth. Pounds."

Icky's jaw dropped. No wonder Dr Lovethang could afford such a frabjous space clinic.

"I haven't got 25 million UK Earth pounds," he peeped.

"Next." barked Dr Lovethang. As his nearest hand stabbed the button to bring up the next ticket number, however, there was a thunderous hammering at the door. Dr Lovethang opened it to reveal a very excited bouncer who, being as he was in the Translation Zone, squealed in perfect English:

"The grotula! A cure for the grotula!"

"How. Can. This. Be?" cried Dr Lovethang.

The bouncer bounced aside, to reveal a wobbly jelly thing almost completely free of red toad-stools. Beside him stood an embarrassed-looking Stinky.

"Show. Me. This. Cure!" demanded Dr Lovethang.

"Do it again!" ordered the bouncer.

Sheepishly, Stinky raised his arm. This was something, as has been mentioned, that Bryan had warned him not to do in public. However, the foul swamp that was Stinky's armpit once again proved to have secret powers. As Dr Lovethang reeled from the pungent stench of pine, onion, skunk and

musk, so the last remaining toadstools vanished from the wobbly thing's feet.

"This. Is. The. Most. Important. Discovery. Since. Cillinillibalonium 3!" declared Dr Lovethang. "You. Can. Put. Down. Your. Arm. Now." he added hastily.

"Sorry," replied Stinky.

"I. Will. Take. A. Sample. Of. The. Juices. Of. Your. Armpit. And. Have. It. Chemically. Analysed." declared Dr Lovethang.

"Hang on," said Icky. "If you want a sample of Stinky's armpit, I want my wound repaired."

Dr Lovethang did a quick calculation. Icky's repair, 25 million UK Earth pounds … cure for Grotula, roughly 950 trillion zillion UK Earth pounds.

"You. Strike. A. Hard. Bargain." he pronounced, offering Icky a hand to shake while another hastily scribbled a contract.

The deal made, Stinky was taken to a nearby cubicle to have his sweat removed while Dr Lovethang prepared to operate on Icky. Icky was the kind of person who liked to watch operations, even on himself, but the doctor moved at such blinding speed it was hard to see what was happening. First the blood was mopped with a mini-vacuum and the wound cleaned with a huff of freezing breath. Then something went into the wound, something small and shiny and white – probably some kind of antibiotic tablet, Icky supposed. Finally all the doctor's arms worked together in a frantic superfast sewing action, like some kind of intergalactic spider weaving a web. In no more than an earth-minute the operation was complete and the wound dressed in a silky bandage which went round Icky's middle like a cummerbund (look it up).

"Do. Not. Remove. Dressing. One. Month." ordered the doctor. "Next!"

Icky tried to look Dr Lovethang in the eyes to thank him, but most were still roving around, and the few on the doctor's face seemed to be deliberately avoiding him. There was nothing left to do but reunite himself with Stinky and get back home in time for breakfast.

# Chapter Nine

It was eerily quiet back at the House of Fun, but not for long. The front door slammed, familiar footsteps marched in, and there was a cry of "OK, Gryan. I'm going to give you one last chance. You can thank your lucky stars that my stick broke and my hankybag fell in a puddle."

The footsteps tramped off up the stairs. Icky turned to Stinky with an urgent expression.

"Stinky!" he hissed. "Where did you put Gryan?"

Stinky pondered a moment. "Ah yes," he said. "The sideboard."

"What sideboard?" quizzed Icky.

"The one in the Living Living Room," replied Stinky.

Icky gave a look of horror. "The Living Living

Room?" he repeated. "You put Gryan in the Living Living Room?"

"Is that bad?" asked Stinky.

"Anything could happen to him in the Living Living Room!" cried Icky.

**Note from Blue Soup**
Fans of the House of Fun will know how true this is. New readers will soon get the idea.

Icky and Stinky hurried to the Living Living Room, where there were the usual creaks and groans from restless furniture and excited squeaks from Dronezone, the frabjous boy band which had been turned into potatoes. The sideboard, however, was quiet – ominously quiet. It was a long low affair with three sliding doors, covered in a garish teak veneer which had looked very modern in the 1960s. Anxiously, Stinky slid open the left-hand door to reveal, to his relief, exactly what he'd put there – a doubled-up dummy with dead staring eyes.

"Let's get him up to my room," said Icky. "We can find some boots for him there."

Stinky held Gryan to his bosom so that the dummy's head looked back over Stinky's shoulder like a baby being winded. The housemates crept from the room with fairy footsteps and began to climb the stairs. Just as they reached the first landing, however, there was a familiar cry:

*"Gottla geer!"*

The housemates stopped dead.

"Did you just do that?" asked Icky.

"I thought it was you," replied Stinky.

"It *was* you!" said Icky.

"It *was* you!" said Stinky.

*"Gottla geer!"* said the voice.

"Saw your lips move that time!" said Icky.

"Really?" replied Stinky.

"No," said Icky.

"Something's wrong here," said Stinky. Slowly, fearfully, he held Gryan Grain out to arm's length. For a moment all was still and silent. Then …

*"Gottla geer!"*

"WERRRRRRRRR!" said Stinky.

"NOOOOOOOOO!" cried Icky.

Stinky's hands lost their grip and Gryan clattered to the ground, ending in a scrumpled knot on the floor. For a moment, again, there was stillness and silence. Then, ever-so-slowly, Gryan uncoiled one arm, pressed his hand to the floor, and before the housemates' horrified eyes, began to struggle to his feet. His first attempt ended in an undignified collapse, but he tried again, and again, until finally he was upright, whereupon he slid on his non-existent foot and clattered once more to the ground.

Something in the housemates told them they should be helping Gryan. Something else hoped the whole nightmare would go away and the helpless dummy return.

As it was, Gryan Grain needed no assistance. Gripping on to a water pipe, he eased himself upward for a second time, and this time held his footing. Steadily, painfully, Gryan forced his good foot forward and began, rather woefully, to hobble towards Icky and Stinky.

*Clunk ... scrape. Clunk ... scrape.*

Suddenly there was an ear-piercing shriek from behind the housemates. "Gryan! You're ... you're *alive!*"

Gryan Grain stopped in his tracks and looked Bryan straight in the eyes.

*"Can I have a glinking gottla geer now?"* he said.

# Chapter Ten

Bryan actually made little fuss about Gryan's burnt stump. What did one missing foot matter when your best friend had come miraculously to life? Gryan had obviously had a mishap resulting from being able to walk – maybe he'd strayed into a bonfire, or stood on a firework as it was about to go off. Gryan didn't remember what had happened and the unfortunate accident was best forgotten.

In any case, there was so much to do! So many pleasures to enjoy together, so many intelligent conversations to be had! Bryan had spent so much time with Icky and Stinky, he had almost forgotten what it was like to discuss the finer points of Beethoven's Fifth Symphony, the beauty of ballet, or the importance of good punctuation.

Gryan was a wonderful learner, attentive to everything Bryan said. He sat patiently on Bryan's knee as Bryan leafed through Postage Stamps of the World, 1896–1954, and when Bryan's favourite classical music was playing, the two sat at opposite ends of the room in identical poses, chins resting on thumbs and finger-ends pressed together in a cradle of Deep Thought. Most importantly, Gryan learned Bryan's jokes word for word as they rehearsed the routine which would surely save the House of Fun.

Icky and Stinky steered well clear of it all. Hopefully, the more time Bryan and Gryan spent alone, the better their act would get. Besides, Icky and Stinky had their own act to think about.

"I know," said Stinky. "You stand against a board and I throw knives all round you."

"Will they be real knives?" asked Icky.

"I'm not sure," replied Stinky.

"Let's avoid anything you're not sure about," suggested Icky.

"That's everything," complained Stinky.

"We could cover ourselves in grease and roll around in feathers," suggested Icky, "then go into the audience and read someone's mind."

Stinky wasn't convinced.

"I could rollerskate round holding a tambourine," suggested Icky, "then you could bite on it and I could swing you round by your teeth."

Stinky was even less convinced.

"We could sing 'Mule Train' and smash trays against our heads," said Icky. "I saw a man do that once."

"We don't know the words," replied Stinky.

"We could make them up," said Icky.

"Does it hurt?" asked Stinky.

"Didn't seem to hurt him," replied Icky.

"Maybe he had a thin tray," suggested Stinky.

"Or a thick head," suggested Icky.

"Let's do it," they chorused.


### Note from Blue Soup

At this point I'm supposed to issue the usual warning about not trying this yourselves at home, but frankly, anyone stupid enough to smash a tray against their head is probably too stupid to be reading a book.

Icky and Stinky's search for trays had hardly begun when they were interrupted by an excited Bryan. He declared that he and Gryan were ready to perform, and that Icky and Stinky should sit on the two chairs specially arranged for the purpose, and say nothing, just laugh and applaud in the right places.

Icky and Stinky duly sat on the chairs, and the performance began.

"Good evening everybody!" pronounced Bryan. "Is there anyone here from Nottingham?"

Silence.

"That's good," declared Bryan, "because I hate knots in my ham!"

More silence. Stinky began to worry.

"Allow me to introduce," cried Bryan, "my little friend Gryan!"

Gryan bowed in all directions, then let out a humungous burp. Icky laughed, Stinky felt less worried, and Bryan looked genuinely surprised.

"I've very sorry," he said. "We didn't rehearse that."

Gryan gurped again. Icky laughed again. Bryan began to look quite peeved. "We will *now*,"

he declared, "do the act we *rehearsed*." He picked up a glass of water and held it on high. "I shall drink this glass of water," he pronounced, "while Gryan recites 'Oh For The Wings of a Dove'."

Bryan duly began to drink the water. Gryan began to recite 'Oh For the Wings of a Dove'. It really was quite impressive. Half way through the recitation, however, Gryan seemed to lose track. The words became garbled, then his voice trailed off completely. Just as the act seemed to be floundering, however, Gryan came back to life to tell the rudest joke any of the housemates had ever heard, complete with huge gestures and even huger swearwords. Bryan spluttered into his water, then clamped his hand over Gryan's mouth.

"I'm *very* sorry!" he declared. "I don't know what's got into him!"

By now Icky and Stinky were rolling about. "That was *gonk*!" cried Icky. "Do it again!"

"It's not what we rehearsed!" complained Bryan.

"Keep it in!" cried Stinky.

"We will *not* keep it in," declared Bryan. "We will go back into rehearsal and Gryan will learn his words properly."

At this, Bryan swept off the stage, his disgraced friend dangling over his arm, still with a smirk on his face. Soon stern words were heard from Bryan's room, followed by meek little replies from Gryan. Obviously Bryan's telling-off was having the desired effect.

Half an hour later, the great double act reappeared. Icky and Stinky were ordered to their seats and the whole thing began again.

"Is anyone here from Birmingham?" asked Bryan.

"Just get on with it," said Icky.

Bryan took up his glass of water, and once more Gryan began to recite 'Oh For The Wings Of A Dove'. This time everything seemed to be going to plan. Bryan sipped, Gryan spoke, and the audience began to feel ever-so-slightly bored. Suddenly, however, completely out of the blue, Gryan stopped dead, lifted one leg, and released the most humungous farrago. The glass dropped clean out of Bryan's hand and the housemates howled with laughter.

"Stop laughing!" cried Bryan. "You're encouraging him!"

"But it's funny!" cried Icky.

"Do you think the Spoonheads will find it funny?" barked Bryan.

"Why not?" asked Icky.

"*Why not?*" blathered Bryan. "Because you can't just *do things like that!*"

"Who says?" replied Icky. "All the grown-ups have gone."

"You can't just do things like that!" repeated Bryan, stamping his foot, seizing his disgraced sidekick and once more departing the stage.

**Note from Blue Soup**

It was of course true that all the grown-ups had been removed from Earth, but Bryan, and many others, still secretly feared that a bolt of lightning might strike from the sky if they did or said certain things. This was despite the fact that the Spoonheads, who lived in the sky, had assured everybody that there was no Big Guy up there moving things round and striking people down, even ones as annoying as Bryan.

# Chapter Eleven

Regular readers of the House of Fun will know all about Bryan's malted milk biscuits and the terrible accident which once befell his head because of them. If you leaf back to Chapter Five you will note how, in a moment of stress, Bryan's first thought was of these biscuits, which in many ways had taken the place of his beloved mother.

However, Bryan had not actually eaten a malted milk biscuit for several months. This was because of a New Year's resolution to give them up due to the fact his teeth were rotting from all the sugar.

It was not easy for Bryan to keep this resolution, so the housemates had agreed that, when particularly upset, Bryan could suck on the edge of a malted milk providing he didn't actually swallow.

This he did on the night of his first performances with Gryan, several times, each time carefully putting the soggy biscuits back in the packet and leaving them in a warm place to dry out.

Icky and Stinky supervised Bryan's biscuit-sucking throughout the evening and were satisfied that no swallowing had taken place. They only went to bed after Bryan had retired and the packet of biscuits was seen to be complete. Imagine their surprise therefore to come down in the morning and find an empty wrapper on the floor, crumbs strewn everywhere and not a malted milk biscuit in sight.

"Bryan!" yelled Icky. "You broke your resolution!"

Bryan clattered into the kitchen, his face flushed and his surprise quite genuine. "I never touched them!" he cried, dropping to his knees and clutching at the empty packet. "You!" he cried. "You had them!"

"We did not so!" protested Icky.

"Right!" said Bryan. "We'll go down to Yellow Mist and find a strange piper who makes us dance the Dance of Truth!"

"Hang on," said Stinky. "Hasn't this already happened?"

Icky huffed impatiently. "If it wasn't Bryan," he said, "isn't it obvious who took the biscuits?"

"Not to me," replied Bryan.

"Gryan!" cried Icky. "Gryan took them!"

"That's a very serious accusation," said Bryan.

With perfect timing, Gryan appeared at the doorway, wearing the same meaningless smile he always wore.

"There are crumbs around his mouth!" cried Icky.

Icky was right. There were indeed crumbs around Gryan's mouth, and quite a few over his jacket as well.

Bryan's manner changed. His head sank. "It's my fault," he murmured. "I forgot to give him his bottle last night."

"You give him a bottle?" said Stinky.

"Every living thing needs fuel," replied Bryan.

"A bottle of what?" asked Icky.

"Beer, of course," replied Bryan.

"What – real beer?" asked Stinky.

"Of course not!" replied Bryan. "Giving him real beer would be a bad influence on young children and suggest that drinking alcohol was somehow big or clever."

## Note from Blue Soup

Have you got that, readers?

"I think real beer might be safer, if it's my ginger beer you're talking about," said Icky.

"Maybe the ginger beer made him go crazy," suggested Stinky.

"He has not gone crazy!" insisted Bryan. "He's just had a bad turn."

"He's had nothing but bad turns," replied Icky.

"I don't see *your act* coming on very well!" snapped Bryan, departing the kitchen in a huff, which is a small furry skateboard-type vehicle which runs on compressed air.

Stinky watched the empty space where Bryan had been, then turned to Icky.

104

"How *is* our act getting along?" he asked.

"I've made up the words," replied Icky.

"Go on," said Stinky.

"Give us the tray," said Icky.

Stinky handed Icky the tray they'd found in the Unwanted Guest Bedroom. It was thin and silver and satisfyingly noisy. Icky held it firmly in his left hand, wound himself up, then began to wail at the top of his voice, smashing the tray lustily against his head at the end of every line.

"Mu-ule TRAIN!

Coming down the DONKEY TRACK!

Mu-ule TRAIN!

See the asses on the BACK!"

Icky wound back down, his left arm hanging limply by his side while the right rubbed furiously at his head. "That hurt," he complained.

"It'll be even worse when you take the space helmet off," replied Stinky.

"That's true," said Icky.

"Good words though," noted Stinky.

Icky looked round at the Kitchen of Magical Invention and began to look quite depressed. "We've had some great adventures here," he said.

"That's true," replied Stinky.

"I don't want to leave," said Icky.

"We're not going anywhere," replied Stinky. "We'll practise and practise till Mule Train is the greatest ever."

"But it's not just up to us," said Icky. "It's up to Bryan. We're depending on Bryan. Except we can't."

"It'll be fine," said Stinky. "You wait. It'll be *ducks deluxe*."

Icky Bats, the world's greatest optimist, was not so sure.

# Chapter Twelve

The day of judgement had seemed to arrive so fast. Bryan peered out nervously on to a sea of expectant faces, and in the centre of the front row, the dreaded Spoonbot. The Spoonbot looked nothing like Bryan had expected. More than anything it resembled a rabbit, a white, hairless rabbit with blank black eyes, focussed remorselessly on the two tense figures on stage.

"Anyone here from Clapham?" trilled Bryan.

No response. Bryan turned anxiously to his faithful sidekick. "Hit them with the song, Gryan," he whispered.

There was no reply. Had Gryan frozen in the lights? Desperately, Bryan urged him to perform, and at that moment noticed something very disturbing.

In the rush of getting ready for the performance, Bryan had somehow forgotten to dress Gryan in his jacket. Not only his jacket – his shirt as well. In fact, Gryan was nothing but a bare wooden dummy.

Now Bryan caught sight of his own forearm. "That's funny," he thought. "I don't remember putting on a short-sleeved shirt."

Bryan's eyes roved further up his arm. As he soon discovered, his shirt had no arms at all. Was he just wearing a vest?

Fearfully, Bryan looked down. No vest.

Even more fearfully, Bryan looked further down ...

Oh no! It had happened again! Completely naked in front of a crowd of people!

At this point Bryan's eyes opened.

"The cheesy dreams bedroom!" he cried. "I fell asleep in the stupid cheesy dreams bedroom!"

Bryan pulled on his clothes and stormed downstairs, leaving Gryan in the Moses basket which was always placed next to Bryan's bed.

"I hate that cheesy dreams bedroom!" he cried, disturbing Icky and Stinky's usual breakfast of cherry dumplings.

"Why did you sleep there then?" asked Icky.

"Because," snapped Bryan, "there was a spider in my room."

"You're never scared of a spider!" laughed Stinky.

Bryan placed both hands on his hips and fixed Stinky with his deadliest stare. "The only reason you don't mind spiders," he declared, "is because you know nothing about them."

"I know there's no poison ones in this house," replied Stinky.

"As a matter of fact," snapped Bryan, "all spiders carry venom. That is how they kill their prey. What is more, the venom also liquidises the prey's innards, after which the spider sucks out their juices and leaves a pitiful withered husk. Personally, I think that is ample reason to dislike spiders."

"What's that noise?" asked Icky, who, as usual, had not been listening to a word Bryan had been saying.

The housemates fell silent, and became aware of a series of muffled thuds and crashes from upstairs.

"Are the pigs attacking again?" asked Stinky, who had never got over the events described in *Stinky Finger's House of Fun*.

"We'd better find out!" said Icky.

The housemates thundered up the stairs towards the noise, which was getting more extreme by the second.

"It's coming from … the cheesy dreams bedroom!" cried Icky.

The housemates clattered to the said room, threw open the door, and were met by a most disturbing and dramatic sight. The room had been totally laid waste, the fridge upended, the walls battered, the bed smashed to bits. And there in the middle of it all, wielding the remains of a metal bedside lamp, was Gryan – still with the same meaningless smile and middle-distance stare.

"Gryan!" gasped Bryan. "Wh-what have you done?"

Gryan's only response was to hand Bryan the broken lamp and amble-hobble calmly from the room.

"What a mess," said Stinky.

"I don't know what came over him," said Bryan.

Icky's eyes narrowed. "*You* said you hated the room," he declared, "then *he* smashed it up."

"I never told him to smash it up!" protested Bryan.

"You never needed to!" cried Icky. "Because Gryan does what he knows you want to do!"

"Balderdash," replied Bryan.

"Yes!" cried Icky. "That's it! *You* really wanted to eat the biscuits!"

"Poppycock," replied Bryan.

"And swear on stage, and tell dirty jokes!" continued Icky.

"This really is going too far," insisted Bryan. But even as he said it, a guilty blush came over his face. There was a few moments' silence, while the truth of Icky's observation sank in.

"We better do something," said Stinky, "before Gryan wrecks the house."

"And the show," added Icky.

"Bryan's got to stop having secret wishes," said Stinky.

"How ridiculous!" snapped Bryan. "How can people stop having secret wishes, not that I have got secret wishes, but if I did have secret wishes, I probably wouldn't even know what they were!"

"There's only one way to find out," said Icky.

"And that is?" asked Bryan, scornfully.

"Hypnosis," replied Icky.

Bryan gave a derisive snort, while Stinky wondered exactly what made noses hip.

"Remember the girls in the Brain Drain van?" said

Icky. "They've got a friend who does hypnosis."

"I am not having hypnosis!" snapped Bryan.

"Bryan, the show is three days away!" cried Icky. "You can't go on stage not knowing what Gryan's going to do!"

"It'll be all right," replied Bryan, not very convincingly.

"Thing is, Bryan," said Icky, "Gryan could reveal anything about you. Anything at all."

Bryan fell silent.

"You haven't got any *more* secret thoughts, have you, Bryan?" asked Stinky.

Bryan's eyes moved rapidly from side to side. "All right!" he snapped. "I'll have the stupid hypnosis! Now don't say I never do anything for you!"

"I'll pixt the Brain Drain van," said Icky.

### Note from Blue Soup

Pixting, of course, is the most brilliant form of communication ever developed. However, I will not explain it, and for a very good reason. Many of these stories have been sent back through the Time Envelope and are being read by people still living in the Dark Ages, the time before the Spoonheads came when the world was run by Money and very nearly destroyed because of it. If people from the Dark Ages learn about pixting they will undoubtedly try to turn it into a Business and therefore create even more chaos. I am here to tell stories, not create chaos.

Now back to this story, which has moved on one day and is about to feature the legendary Erin Yinka Rose.

All three housemates hurried to the front door. It was the moment Bryan had been dreading and Icky and Stinky eagerly awaiting. The door opened to reveal a girl, just like the housemates had expected, except for one thing: she was rather attractive, with caramel skin and deep dark eyes that crinkled as she smiled, as did the corners of her mouth, so it seemed as if her smile also had a smile. Her manner was calm and businesslike, but there was a glimmer of warmth behind it, like a nice cake inside a filing cabinet.

"And which of you is Bryan?" she asked, with a voice that matched her eyes.

Bryan raised a sheepish hand.

"I am Erin Yinka Rose," announced the girl. "You can call me Erin. We'll need a suitably quiet place, somewhere you feel comfortable."

"Would you like a cup of tea?" asked Icky, completely ignoring what Erin had just said.

"Or a bite of my sandwich?" asked Stinky. "I've only had a couple of mouthfuls."

"I'll just get on with the job, thank you," replied Erin.

Bryan led Erin to the Super Safari Lounge where they were quickly joined by Gryan. Bryan selected a peaceful view of some bubbling geysers in Iceland, then took a seat with Gryan on his lap.

"Do we have to have the doll?" asked Erin.

"He's not a doll," replied Bryan. "He's my friend."

"Hmm" said Erin. She made a note in her note-book, then sat opposite Bryan and looked him steadily in the eyes. "I want you to keep your eyes fixed on mine," she said, "and relax completely."

"I have to warn you," replied Bryan, "that I have a very strong mind which cannot easily be influenced. For examp—"

"That's it," said Erin. "You're under."

Bryan said nothing, just sagged a little.

"I want you to go back," said Erin, "to a time when you were really upset."

"Dentist," mumbled Bryan, without a second thought.

"What about the dentist, Bryan?" asked Erin.

"I'm scared, Daddy!" wailed Bryan. "I don't want the dentist to take my tooth out!"

Erin's next question was cut short as Bryan leapt to his feet, suddenly holding forth in a gruff dark growl: *"Bryan, I've told you a hundred times! Papa or father, never daddy!"*

"I'm scared, father!" cried Bryan, in his normal voice.

*"Pull yourself together, there's a good boy."*

"I want a cuddle, father!"

*"There's no call for that kind of talk."*

"Please, father! Please give me a cuddle!"

*"I'll give you a handshake."*

"I don't want a handshake, father! I want a cuddle!"

*"Bryan, that is enough! Here, take this biscuit and we'll hear no more of it!"*

"Bicky ... bicky ... num num num num num num num num ..."

Bryan's voice trailed off, though the chewing motions continued for a some while, eventually concluding with a determined swallow followed by a glum stare into the middle distance.

"Hmm," said Erin to herself. "I think we may have our work cut out here." She addressed Bryan firmly. "Bryan," she announced, "I am going to click my fingers, and when I do, you will be back in the room with me."

Erin clicked her fingers. Bryan jolted back to reality, then shook his head sadly. "Knew it wouldn't work," he said.

"I had to bring you back," said Erin. "We were getting into dangerous territory."

"I beg your pardon?" said Bryan.

"I'd prefer your friend to leave," said Erin.

"I wouldn't," said Bryan, who had never been alone with any girl, let alone a hypnotising one.

"In that case," said Erin, "the session is over."

"We haven't even started!" said Bryan.

"When you're ready for a one-on-one session, without your friend, pixt me," said Erin, firmly.

Bryan didn't know what to say. He really didn't want Erin to go, but the thought of being stuck on his own with her filled him with panic. They returned to the entrance hall, where Icky and Stinky were waiting eagerly.

"What happened?" quizzed Icky.

"I'll write a full report," replied Erin.

"But we've got to know Bryan's secret wishes!" protested Icky.

"Goodbye, Bryan," said Erin.

"Bye," Bryan mumbled, into his non-existent beard.

At this point the scene seemed to be over, were it not for the fact that Gryan had left Bryan's side and was making his way, slowly and steadily, towards Erin. Finally reaching her, he held up his arms like a hopeful baby. Not knowing what else to do, Erin picked him up, whereupon he brought his little wooden face towards hers and planted a big fat wooden kiss on her cheek. Rather shocked, Erin returned Gryan to the floor, hastily repeated her farewell, and exited.

All eyes fell on Bryan, who had blushed as red as burning coal. "Wh-what did you do that for?" he demanded of Gryan.

"You love her!" cried Icky, in sheer delight.

"Piffle!" cried Bryan.

"You wanted to kiss her!" cried Icky.

"Tommyrot!" cried Bryan. "I hate her! I hate all girls!"

"Br-yan's got a girl-friend! Br-yan's got a girl-friend!" sang Icky and Stinky.

Bryan looked into his housemates' joyful jeering faces and his own expression sank into a scowl as deep and dark as the ocean floor. "That feeling," he growled. "It's come back."

"What, the loving feeling?" laughed Icky.

"The feeling," replied Bryan, "that someone is about to die."

# Chapter Thirteen

Icky had also been having a strange feeling lately, but it was more of an itchy feeling, and it came from his stitched-up wound. He hadn't actually seen the wound since it had been repaired, as Dr Lovethang had told him very firmly not to remove the silken dressing. Icky wasn't sure which was worse – the itch, or not being able to look. Either way, it kept him awake that night, which meant of course that he had to wake up Stinky. Bleary-eyed, Stinky was dragged down to the kitchen for the usual game of battleships and discussions about Life in General – the kind of discussions you only have at midnight, and always forget by morning.

After just a few minutes of this meaningless discussion, however, the housemates were halted by a familiar noise. It was the unmistakeable sound of Gryan making his way downstairs.

"I think he's going to the Time-travel Garage," said Stinky.

"Why should he go to the Time-travel Garage?" asked Icky.

"Maybe he needs the time-travel van," suggested Stinky.

"Or a tool," suggested Icky.

"Why should Gryan need a tool?" asked Stinky.

Icky pondered for a few seconds, then a look of great certainty came over him. "Bryan's spider," he replied. "Gryan's getting a tool to kill Bryan's spider."

"What kind of tool would he use to kill a spider?" asked Stinky.

"A spider wrench?" suggested Icky.

"I've seen those on the web," replied Stinky.

"Ssh!" said Icky. "I think he's coming this way."

The housemates listened closely.

*Clunk ... scrape. Clunk ... scrape. Clunk ... scrape.*

Yes, Gryan was definitely heading their way.

"I'm getting a bad feeling about this," said Stinky.

"Shall we lock the door?" suggested Icky.

"Yeah," replied Stinky.

Icky rushed to the door. "Where's the key?" he gasped.

"I put it somewhere for safe-keeping," replied Stinky.

"*Where?*" cried Icky.

"Dunno," replied Stinky. "Hasn't this happened before?"

*Clunk … scrape. Clunk … scrape. Clunk …*

Icky backed away.

For a moment, the house was silent.

Then **SLAMMMMM!**

The door crashed into the wall. In the open doorway stood Gryan Grain, murder in his eyes, a woodsman's axe in his hands.

"Y-you want to be careful with that, Gryan," stammered Stinky.

Gryan's only answer was to advance two paces and swing the axe with extreme force. The kitchen bread-bin was reduced to splinters.

"S-see what I mean?" stammered Stinky.

Gryan advanced another two paces and swung again. This time it was curtains for the egg-timer.

123

Icky's eyes fell on the bottle of surgical spirit, which, as he now realised, was sulphuric acid. Beside it, as chance would have it, was a bicycle pump.

Gryan advanced another pace.

Keeping one eye on the deadly doll, Icky opened the bottle of acid, sucked the contents into the bike pump, and handed the loaded pump to

Stinky. "Here, Stinky," he said. "You're a good aim."

"What do you want me to do?" asked Stinky.

"When I say," replied Icky, "fire it at his hands."

"Got you," said Stinky, none too confidently.

Gryan advanced two more paces, almost within touching distance, then in a sudden sinister arc swung the axe high above his head.

"Now!" cried Icky.

Stinky fired his makeshift weapon, sending a scorching jet of acid towards Gryan. The effort propelled Stinky backwards, tumbling to the floor. "Did I get him?" he gasped.

"You missed his hands!" cried Icky. "You missed his hands ... and got his face!"

Stinky jolted upright just in time to see the ghastly sight of Gryan, still careering towards them, a great smoking hole where his nose and mouth used to be.

"Quick, Stinky!" cried Icky, grabbing his great mate by the arm. "Run!"

But where? The back door led to outer space, and there was no way past Gryan into the rest of the house. The only option was those two sliding doors in the corner of the room marked GM, and GM, as you all know, stood for that terrifying transport system in the very bowels of the house — the Ghost Metro.

Icky yanked the lever that opened the door. Behind it was not an escalator but a small old-fashioned lift with a sign saying MAXIMUM WEIGHT FIVE PERSONS OR SEVEN PIGS. Icky and Stinky piled into the lift and pressed the CLOSE DOORS button, but just as the doors were sealing tight, a small wooden arm forced its way between them.

"Press Go!" yelled Icky.

"But … his arm …" babbled Stinky.

This was no time for sentiment. Icky pressed the button marked B for basement, there was a creak, a judder, and the lift began to sink downwards, with the arm still trapped in the doors. Not for long, however. As the lift dropped below floor level, there was a sickening snap and a severed wooden arm clattered on to the floor beside them. Stinky viewed this with alarm, as if it might leap up and grab him by the throat, but Icky's mind was focussed on the other horrors ahead.

It wasn't long before the two housemates were

facing these horrors. As the doors slid open, Icky stepped straight into the rotting guts of one of the many zombies which populated the metro. The cold putrid gloop went right over the top of his shoes and through his socks. "That's rancid!" he cried.

It was a fatal distraction. The housemates had forgotten to jam the lift doors, and in a second these had closed behind them. That meant the lift was returning to the kitchen.

"Quick!" cried Icky. "We've got to get to Bryan's room!"

Icky and Stinky leapt the nearest turnstile and pounded down the dark dripping tunnels towards the platforms. As all fans of the House of Fun will know, the ghost metro was a huge warren which bore no relation to the size of the house above. Getting to Bryan's room would involve getting at least one train and possibly two, and almost certainly going via Cockfosters on the Pigsick and Gurgle line.

What made the situation even more eerie was that the housemates could hear music. A jangling guitar was echoing down the dismal tunnels, and the further they ran, the louder it got. Suddenly, turning a corner, they came face to face with a pair of gangling skeletons, each with a guitar strapped around its fleshless shoulder.

"Oh no," groaned Stinky. "Not skeleton buskers."

"*And* they're playing 'The Streets of London'," moaned Icky. "That song sucks."

The housemates slowed to a walk. The skeletons didn't seem to be looking at them, but it was hard to tell, seeing as they only had eye sockets. However, the head of one was tilted up as if lost in the music, while the other seemed to be focussed on a dark woollen cap on the floor, in which were scattered a few coins.

"Walk slowly," commanded Icky.

The housemates crept forward. There was no response from the skeletons.

"When I say Now," whispered Icky, "you go like hell one side, I'll go the other."

"OK," whispered Stinky.

"Now!" cried Icky.

Just as planned, Icky and Stinky ran like hell. Unfortunately, however, Icky had not made it clear exactly which side was One and which the Other. As a result they both hared straight into the same narrow space, crashed into one another, and in the next instant found themselves seized by two pairs of skeleton hands and slowly drawn tight to the skeleton buskers' bony ribs. It was a truly horrible experience to have a hand of bones clamped across your face, but what made it worse was a familiar spooky sound behind them in the tunnel:

*Clunk ... scrape. Clunk ... scrape. Clunk ... scrape.*

"Let us go!" cried Icky, his voice muffled by the gag of bones across his mouth.

There was no reply.

*Clunk ... scrape. Clunk ... scrape. Clunk ... scrape.*

"What do you want with us?" cried Icky.

There was no reply.

*Clunk ... scrape. Clunk ... scrape. Clunk ... scrape.*

"The gore police are coming!" cried Icky.

But it was not the gore police (whoever they were) which turned the corner at that moment. It was Gryan Grain, deadly doll of death, now footless, faceless and with just one arm, swinging the razor-sharp axe with even more ferocity than before. Slowly, remorselessly, he bore down on the two housemates, seized like two nails in a vice, helpless.

It was at this point that Icky had an idea. If he could just force one hand into his pocket ... pull out a few coins ...

... drop them into the hat ...

Magic! No sooner had the coins landed than the skeleton buskers relaxed their grip. Icky and Stinky were free. They pelted off down the tunnel towards the train line while the deadly doll hacked thin air.

**Note from Blue Soup**

Next time you see some poor busker in the Underground or on the street, perhaps you will remember this scene.

130

If Icky and Stinky believed the worst was over, however, they had another think coming. The electronic sign above the station platform told them there was two minutes till the next train – time enough for even a one-legged dummy to catch it.

"Come *on!*" urged Icky, who was impatient at the best of times, let alone the worst of them.

"We need a weapon," said Stinky. His eyes fell on a long-handled broom. Unfortunately this was in the grip of a station attendant whose other arm carried his head.

*Clunk … scrape. Clunk … scrape. Clunk … scrape.*

"Come *on!*" cried Icky.

Mercifully, the train appeared at the end of the tunnel. At the same time, however, the deadly doll hobbled on to the platform and caught sight of the housemates. Gryan Grain was slow, but so, for some reason, was the train – deadly slow.

*Clunk … scrape. Clunk … scrape. Clunk … scrape.*

Stinky had to get that broom. With a brief apology he grabbed the business end of it, but its owner was not giving it up lightly. Luckily for Stinky, however, the attendant only had one style of fighting – the headbutt. This didn't work half as well with your head tucked under your arm. As Stinky came away with the broom, so the head flew out of the attendant's grasp, rolled around the platform, then dropped on to the live rail, where it fizzed and popped like a firework. It then disappeared beneath the train which ground and squealed to a halt just past Icky and Stinky.

"Quick, Stinks!" yelled Icky. "Jump on!"

"No good!" cried Stinky. "Gryan'll get on too!"

With that, Stinky turned to face the deadly doll, now just metres away. Taking aim carefully with the broom, Stinky lurched forward and swept – once, twice, once again. All misses.

Gryan Grain's one arm swiped through the air. His deadly axe took the head of the broom clean off.

Stinky swept again. Contact! Gryan staggered towards the edge of the platform. Seizing his chance, Stinky summoned all his strength for one telling blow. The blow caught Gryan's one good leg, sending him toppling to the ground, rolling twice, then – hallelujah! – tumbling off the platform edge. There was a crack like thunder as the axe hit the live rail, then Gryan disappeared into a cloud of sparks

132

and smoke. For a moment Stinky stood rooted to the spot, then Icky yanked him into the end carriage of the train. The doors creaked shut, the train gave a jolt, and the housemates began to move away, heaving sighs of relief.

"You're a hero, Stinky," declared Icky.

"Thanks," replied Stinky, "but I still feel kind of bad."

The two mates fell to silence.

"Hey, Stinky," said Icky, eventually. "Remember when we did electricity at school?"

"I don't even remember school," replied Stinky.

"We learnt all the things that conducted it," said Icky.

"What, like conducting an orchestra?" asked Stinky.

"I mean the things that *carry* electricity," replied Icky. "Like metal and water."

"And wood?" suggested Stinky.

"Not wood," replied Icky. "Wood's what they call a non-conductor."

At that moment Icky and Stinky seemed to have the same thought. They turned towards the back window of the carriage.

# AIEEEEEEEEEEEEEEEE!

The housemates' baleful cry echoed round the Ghost Metro. There, stuck against the window, was the mouthless face of Gryan Grain, now black as soot and bald as a coot. As Icky and Stinky watched in horror, so Gryan's one remaining arm came into view, slowly, painfully, hauling himself up to reveal the axe, stuffed in the remains of his belt and as deadly as ever.

The train was drawing to a halt. It was the stop for Bryan's bedroom. Hearts pumping like pistons, Icky and Stinky leapt off and raced down the exit tunnel towards the escalator. Icky managed to get his pocket caught on the end of this, and without even daring to look behind, ripped the pocket right out of his jacket to get on to the moving stairs. The two of them did not stop for breath one second. They ran all the way up the escalator, pulled the lever that opened the doors at the top, and spilled out into Bryan's room, lungs bursting from the effort.

"Jam the doors!" cried Icky.

Stinky looked around, spied Bryan's badminton racket, and jammed this against the door lever.

None of this woke Bryan. Bryan was out cold, cuddled around a pillow, earplugs in his ears and nightcap over his eyes. On his bedside table was an open notebook, every inch covered in scrawly little hearts.

"Bryan!" yelled Icky, pulling off his nightcap. "You've got to save us!"

Bryan's eyes opened. He frowned. One hand plucked the earplug from his left ear. "I was having a nice dream," he moaned.

"Gryan's trying to kill us!" cried Stinky.

"Maybe you deserve it," grumbled Bryan.

"We're not joking!" cried Icky. "He's got an axe!"

With perfect timing, there was an almighty THUNK, and the head of the said axe smashed through the escalator door. Blow after blow followed, each enough to make the room shake, till an entire section of the door had been smashed through.

135

Nothing in the Ghost Metro could match the sight that followed: Gryan Grain climbing through the smashed door, one-footed, one-armed, faceless, bald and burnt beyond recognition.

"W-what is it?" trembled Bryan.

"It's Gryan, Bryan," replied Stinky.

"W-what happened to him?" asked Bryan.

"Never mind that!" cried Icky. "Stop him!"

This time there really was no exit. Icky and Stinky were backed into a corner, hemmed in by Bryan's bed, with the mad axe dummy still coming, still swinging, still deadly.

"How can I stop him?" pleaded Bryan.

"Stop thinking you want to kill us!" cried Icky.

"But it's a secret thought!" cried Bryan. "I can't just stop thinking it!"

"We're your friends!" cried Stinky.

"But you laughed at me!" cried Bryan.

"We never meant it!" cried Icky.

"You still did it!" cried Bryan.

THUNK! The axe fell on the bedside table, splitting the top in two.

"We're sorry, Bryan!" cried Stinky.

"You don't mean it!" cried Bryan.

"We do!" cried Icky and Stinky together. "We're really sorry!"

Too late! Gryan had reached the housemates. He raised his axe ...

... and froze.

"I must have stopped hating you," said Bryan.

"Wow," said Stinky.

All eyes were on Gryan. For a moment he was deadly still ... then teetered slightly ... then, without warning, crumbled into a pile of cinders, the axe clattering harmlessly alongside.

"Wow," said Stinky again.

"Gryan ..." mumbled Bryan. A single tear formed in his eye, ran, dripped and sizzled in his little friend's still-warm ashes.

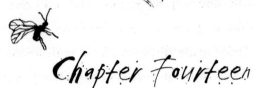

# Chapter Fourteen

Gryan's ashes were put into Bryan's best biscuit tin and buried among the bubbling geysers in the Super Safari Lounge. There was a short, simple ceremony, which should really have been dignified but actually wasn't, since it involved Bryan trying very badly to throw his voice and make the tin speak.

But of course the story was not over yet. There was the small matter of the Greatest Show on Earth, which, if it didn't turn out so great, would become the Show That Sent Icky, Stinky and Bryan to the Space Zoo.

There was no time to change the act. Having said that, Bryan's routine would never work with a pile of ashes sitting on his knee. Only one possibility remained: someone would have to take the place of Gryan, someone preferably with clean trousers. Someone, therefore, called Icky.

Stinky did a fantastic job with the make-up he found in the Dressing-up Room. The red cheeks, the lines running down from the corners of the mouth ... Icky really did look like a ventriloquist's dummy. His only problem was sitting still, especially when the itch in his side was driving him crazy.

But Icky would just have to do his best. The day was upon them, the audience were in their seats, and the glow of pale green light in the front row indicated that the Spoonbot was with them. Stinky drew the curtains apart and Bryan checked for the nineteenth time that he was still wearing his trousers.

"Good evening and welcome!" he croaked. "Anyone here from Cheltenham?"

Dead silence.

"That's good," peeped Bryan, "because I don't like ... don't like ..."

Disaster! Bryan had forgotten his lines already!

"... don't like people from Cheltenham," mumbled Bryan.

There was an embarrassed cough.

"And now," declared Bryan, shakily, "I shall drink a glass of water while my little friend sings 'Mule Train'."

The fingers of Icky's right hand tightened around his silver tray. The itch was now almost enough to make him scream.

"Behold," said Bryan. "The glass."

Stinky handed Bryan his glass of water. He held it to the light, then began to drink. Icky immediately burst into song:

"Mu-ule TRAIN!

Coming down the DONKEY TRACK!

Mu-ule TRAIN!

See the asses on the BACK!"

Unfortunately, however, Icky's itch drove him to smash his head so hard that he completely lost his balance. As a result he fell right off Bryan's knee into a position that was very human and not at all wooden.

There was a boo from the audience. The Spoonbot flickered like a busy memory stick.

At this point, just as it seemed the game was up, something very remarkable began to happen.

Icky's wound started to swell like a balloon, stretching the silken bandage until it snapped. The swelling grew, and grew, till the swelling was almost as big as the rest of Icky, whereupon Icky gave an almighty groan. Suddenly a great long arm broke out of his side, curling like a whip before Bryan's astonished face. This was followed by another arm, then another, then another, till a perfect mini-sized replica of Dr Lovethang detached itself from Icky and dropped into the centre of the stage, while Icky's side re-sealed itself.

To the music of the audience's gasps, the mini doctor then swelled, split its skin, then swelled and split its skin again, each time emerging a different colour. Finally the veins lit up like fairylights beneath its skin and it swept from the room, heading for the exit of the House of Fun and a new life on Earth.

For a moment there was nothing but shock, not least from the housemates. Then the audience burst into rapturous applause, knowing that they, like the Spoonbot, had just witnessed a once-in-a-lifetime performance – a performance so stunning, it could only be called the Greatest Show on Earth.

"Is it sore, Icky?" asked Stinky, as the audience, and the Spoonbot, filed happily from the makeshift theatre.

"Is what sore?" said Icky, who, not surprisingly, was a bit dazed.

Stinky tousled his great friend's hair, and for good measure, gave Bryan a reassuring pat on the shoulder. Then he sat back and closed his eyes, grateful, hopeful and thankful, because nothing makes you appreciate a thing like the threat of losing it.

**More adventures with Stinky and friends!**

## STINKY FINGER'S HOUSE OF FUN

*Jon Blake*

The Spoonheads have arrived in their space-hoovers and sucked up all the grown-ups! So Stinky and Icky will never have to change their underwear again.

In search of an Aim in Life, the two great mates head off to Uncle Nero's House of Fun. But soon they're being besieged by an army of pigs who want to make people pies!

They're going to need more than Icky's lucky feather and Stinky's smelly pants to save their crazy new home ...